IF FEELINGS TAKE OVER

By Danielle Nichols

Printed in the United States of America.

First Printing, 2017

ISBN 978-1548826567

Sounds and Symbols, LLC
PO Box 5392
Englewood, CO 80155

Illustrations are a collaboration between Danielle Nichols and the professionals at Yami (yamishopping.com).

Layout by graphic designer Jeca Novakovic
(www.jecanovakovic.com)

Dedicated to my students

Pre-Reading Discussion Ideas

1. What does it mean to be "calm?" When you are calm, what is your body like? Act it out!

2. What does it mean for something to get "taken over?" (Think about knights taking over a castle.)

3. Do you think you're in control of <u>how</u> you feel? Why or why not? Do you think you're in control of what you <u>do</u> with those feelings? Why or why not?

This is my friend, Mike.
He's in third grade, like me.

He likes science and
soccer and technology.

He starts each day calm
and he doesn't complain,

That's because everything's
calm in his brain.

His thoughts sit
on shelves, each
thought has
its place.

They rest, sit, and
think in their own
little space.

His organized
brain makes him
ready to learn.

He studies and
plays and he waits
for his turn.

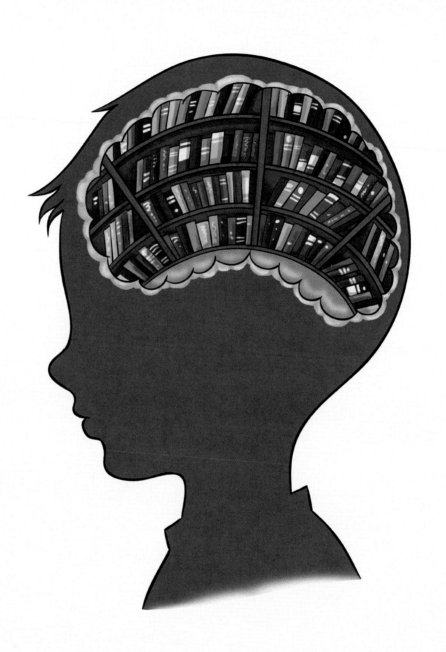

ANGRY

HAPPY

Mike does a lot in a busy school day.
He'll add and he'll write, and at recess, he'll play.

Sometimes he feels neutral, sometimes he feels mad,
Or at the same time he is happy and sad.

SAD

NEUTRAL

Those feelings are also on shelves in his head.
They don't look like books. They are heart-shaped instead.

His feelings and thoughts can work well side by side,
But if feelings get rowdy, hold on for the ride!

If Mike lets his feelings knock thoughts off the shelf,
He can't think quite right, he's no longer himself.

When thoughts in his brain start to tumble and fall,
He can't reason or listen or see straight at all.

If Mike's feelings are wild and his thoughts out of place,
It shows in his body, his words, and his face!

Mike's body gets tight
and then he starts to cry.

He yells things and throws
things and acts like he'll die.

I know he won't die,
he was just doing awesome!

If thoughts fall off shelves,
everything is a problem.

10

We call this a "tantrum." He had one in writing.
He heard the assignment and just started crying.

He would not take help, read a book, take a break.
His yelling and tears gave us all a headache.

Our teacher looked frustrated, even upset,
And as for us kids, were we scared? You bet!

Tantrums make it so he can't play or study,
And I have a hard time just being his buddy.

Most of the time we have fun hanging out,
But during a tantrum, that's it – I am out!

Look at the other kids in the classroom.
Do they notice Mike is having a tantrum?
How does Mike's tantrum make them feel?

I don't think Mike likes when his friends walk away.
If he'd just stay calm, we'd be happy to play!

Managing feelings is kind of confusing,
But with some good help, I could see him improving.

So I asked my teacher if I could help out.
After all, isn't helping what friendship's about?

Our teacher agreed, and we started right then.
"To start calming down," she said, "Please count to ten."

Mike counted out loud while I patted his back.
Calm and ready, we started our plan of attack.

Our teacher told Mike, "First, you must be aware.
Find out how you feel and then we'll go from there."

"Being aware" means you're paying
attention and know what's going on

She got out some paper and pencils for us
And wrote out the subjects that we would discuss.

She asked Mike how he felt in class when we're reading.
He replied, "I feel neutral, I'd rather be eating."

She continued, "Pretend there's a scale, one to ten,
How strong do you feel?" And he thought once again.

He answered, "Four, not too much or too little,"
And our teacher drew hearts just the size of a nickel.

Reading | Ma... | | Writing | History | Science

I jumped in, "Mike, what do you feel during math?"
He said, "Six happy hearts," and we each drew in half.

I asked, "How many hearts do you feel at recess?"
Mike answered, "4 happy, 2 mad, I would guess."

"10 angry for writing," he continued to think.
"Well, angry and nervous. I'm sure they are linked."

We finished our graph and it looked really great!
It's cool to see feelings can be lined up straight.

Our teacher explained, "Those big feelings are fine,
But now let's find tools that can keep them in line!"

When you have a problem, you need the right tool to fix it. If
Mike can't act calmly, he has a problem. What tools could help
Mike keep his feelings from taking over?

"First," she said, "Thinking ahead is a tool.
You'll know what is next, and you'll keep your cool."

Mike realized, "Writing puts me at a ten.
I guess I should start calming down <u>before</u> then."

"Exactly!" our teacher exclaimed with a smile.
"Soon it will be natural, but give it a while."

She said, "If your feelings still bounce off the walls,
Take deep breaths, drink water, go walk in the hall.

And if thoughts in your head tell you something's too tough,
Think, 'That's not true - I can handle this stuff!'"

I told Mike, "You can do this. And I'll be here too.
If you want to talk, I can be there for you."

Mike took a deep breath and he said, "I will try.
It's hard, but I'm glad to have you standing by."

We chose tools to keep all Mike's feelings in line.
(I even took notes to help me deal with mine!)

When he's too excited, he'll breathe to calm down.
When he's sad, he'll drink water, maybe walk around.

When he's mad it's the hardest to follow a plan,
But he starts with a stress ball to squeeze with his hands.

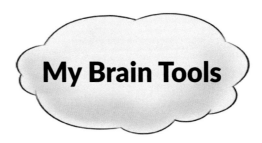

My Brain Tools

- Count to 10
- Think about what's coming next
- Take deep breaths
- Drink water
- Go for a walk (ask teacher first)
- Talk nicely to myself
- Talk to a friend
- Ask a teacher for help

Mike is now ready with plenty of tools
He can use anywhere, like at home and in school.

Tools help his feelings calm down when they're strong.
His thoughts don't fall over – they all get along!

With tools ready to go, Mike will not be the same:
He won't let his feelings take over his brain.

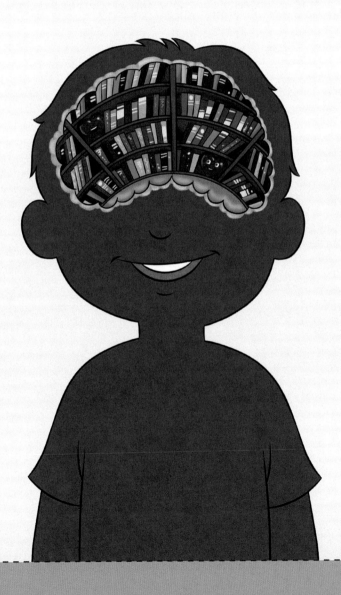

Post-Reading Discussion Ideas

1. When is <u>your</u> brain calm and organized?

2. What are some things that are easier to do when your brain is calm and organized? What are some things that are harder to do when feelings take over?

3. Think about your brain. When do overexcited feelings take over? When do angry feelings take over? When do _____ feelings take over?

4. What do you think about Mike's angry and nervous feelings being linked? How do you think they are linked? Do you ever have two feelings at the same time?

5. What can you do to keep feelings from taking over your brain?

6. How can you plan ahead so you're ready when you have strong feelings?

7. Is it the objects (like a water bottle or stress ball) that make everything better, or is it Mike's thoughtful use of them that helps him manage his emotions?

8. Do you think Mike mastered managing his feelings quickly? Why or why not?

Post-Reading Activity

Copy the following page. Make a bar graph of your feelings using hearts, just like Mike did in the book. Then make a list of tools you can use to keep your feelings from taking over your brain. Ask an adult to help you decide whether the tools will actually help you or if other tools might work better.

Managing My Feelings

My Brain Tools

overexcited

sad

angry

The Science Behind

IF FEELINGS TAKE OVER

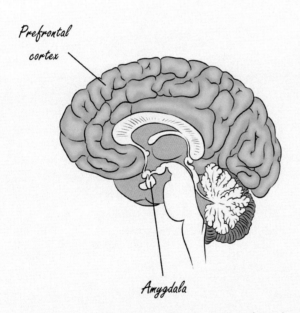

Prefrontal cortex

Amygdala

The prefrontal cortex is the front part of the cerebral cortex (the biggest and outermost part of your brain). It's where you have thoughts you are aware of and can learn to control.

The amygdala is deep inside your brain and pretty small. This is where you have feelings.

You have to use the skills in your prefrontal cortex to keep the amygdala from taking over. The problem is that when feelings take over, it's hard to use your prefrontal cortex! That's why it's important to plan ahead. You can strengthen your prefrontal cortex by being aware of how different things make you feel, checking that you are reacting appropriately to what's going on, and knowing how to positively channel your emotions.

Managing emotions is a tough job, but your brain is ready for the challenge!

Made in the USA
Columbia, SC
05 January 2021